CARROT CAKE

CARROT CAKE

BY NONNY HOGROGIAN

E
HOG

 GREENWILLOW BOOKS

A DIVISION OF WILLIAM MORROW & CO., INC., NEW YORK

1   2   3   4   5   6   7   8   9   10

Library of Congress Cataloging in Publication Data
Hogrogian, Nonny.   Carrot cake.   Summary: The rabbit newlyweds set up housekeeping and learn something important about living together.   [1. Rabbits—Fiction.   2. Marriage—Fiction]   I. Title.
PZ7.H6844Car   [E]   76-17628   ISBN 0-688-80061-0 ISBN 0-688-84061-2 lib. bdg.

Everyone said it was the finest match
in the rabbit kingdom.

C.2

The parents were very happy
and the wedding was an elegant affair.
There was cabbage stew and turnip pie
and lettuce under glass.

When most of the food was eaten,
the young couple prepared to leave
for their honeymoon.
Mother Rabbit kissed her daughter
and told her to love, honor,
and always care for her husband.

The young groom's mother kissed her son.
"Be a kind and loving husband
and never hurt your wife," she said.

After two weeks
the happy newlyweds returned home
and started their life together.

There was cooking to be done
and other chores
inside and out of the rabbit hole.

And they had much to learn
about each other.

One evening after dinner
they went for a stroll in the garden.

"What shall we talk about?" asked Mr. Rabbit.

"I can't think of anything," Mrs. Rabbit answered.

"Well then, I shall tell you about my journey
to town this morning."

"Oh," she said.

"First of all," he said, "I went to the carpenter to have our door repaired."

"Oh," she said again.

"Then," he said, "I bought this new vest
to wear when we go visiting."

"Oh," repeated Mrs. Rabbit.

"Is that all you can say?" said Mr. Rabbit.

"Well, what should I say?" she asked.

"You might say, 'Wear your new vest
with smiles until it falls apart.'"

"Well, if you say so," his shy wife said,
"wear it with smiles until it falls apart."

"That is better," he said.

"Later I gathered enough wood
to keep us warm this winter."

Mrs. Rabbit, wanting to please her husband,
repeated what he told her to say,
"Wear it with smiles until it falls apart."

"No! No! I'm talking about wood.
You should say, 'We shall burn it happily
and keep warm by its fire.'"

"Oh, is that what you think
I should say? We shall burn it happily
and keep warm by the fire."

Mr. Rabbit continued. "Then I filled the cracks
and patched the outer walls of our home.
It is as fine as a new one."

"We shall burn it happily," said Mrs. Rabbit.

"Wife, weren't you listening?
You should say, 'We shall have children
and live in it with joy.'"

"We shall live in it with joy," Mrs. Rabbit muttered.

Mr. Rabbit continued relating
the day's events.
"When I went to gather food
I was caught in a hunter's trap."

"We shall live in it joyously with all our
children," repeated Mrs. Rabbit.

"Not in a trap! You should say,
'Have no fear, our friends would help
to take you out.'"

"Our friends would help to take you out."

"As it happened, I managed to slip out by myself
  and ran to the bakery to pick up the carrot cake.
  I leaned over to sniff the cake
  and the baker almost knocked my eye out
  with his rolling pin."

"Our friends would help to take it out."

"Foolish wife! You should tell the baker
  how senseless he is," Mr. Rabbit shouted.

But the young wife had had enough.
"You senseless rabbit," she said, and she began
to hit him.

"Wife, what are you doing?" Mr. Rabbit cried.

"You keep telling me what to say, but I'm not
as dumb as you think," and she hit him again.

"Oh, oh." It was Mr. Rabbit this time.

"Is that all you can say?" she cried.

"Well, what should I say?"

"You should ask me about *my* day,
and you should be patient with my shyness
or even my stupidity."

She was crying.

"I was so busy talking," Mr. Rabbit said,
"that I didn't stop to think about you."

"Silence is good sometimes, too," said Mrs. Rabbit.

He kissed her and she hugged him
and they strolled back to their rabbit hole
where they happily ate their carrot cake
and didn't try to talk.